My Wonderful Curls

Written By
Tristan Towns &
Lacey Howard

Illustrated By
Whimsical Designs by CJ

First published in 2022
Printed in the United States

Written by: Tristan Towns and Lacey Howard
(IG/FB: @sistersbookcorner)

Illustrations and cover art: Whimsical Designs by CJ

ISBN: 978-1-7379346-0-8 (paperback)

Published by DeSisso Publishing

To all of those with curly hair, no matter your age, may you always embrace your wonderful curls and be proud to be uniquely you!

My curls are unique just like me.

When I look in the mirror, I love what I see!

Hair so big and fluffy, too,
I love my curls and all they do.

Red or blonde, black or brown,
Curls come in all colors. What shade is your crown?

I wear my hair in all kinds of styles.
My curls are so cool and so versatile.

I can wear puffs.

I rock my waves.

I love my twists.

I like my braids.

I can wear my hair in a big fro,
Or style it easy with a wash-n-go.

What styler do I use when my hair starts to frizz?
Gel, cream, or mousse; nothing stops me from rocking this!

To help my curls I deep condition.
It gives them moisture and lots of nutrition.

Clippers on the sides for my high top fade,
On top, my curls are out in full display.

Curls piled high up in a bun.
My curly hair shines just like the sun.

I love to sit in my barber's chair,
And watch the magic he does with my hair.

How do I style my curls at night?

Up in a pineapple to keep my curls right.

Our curly hair is different, and that's okay.
We both wear our curls in our own special way.

I shake my ringlets out. I wear my coils proud.
My curly hair stands out in the crowd.

No curly hair day is ever the same,
But I love my amazing curly mane!

Having curls is no problem when I'm playing sports,
I wear my curls proudly on the field or court.

My curls have lots of volume, and I love it that way.
The bigger the better is what I always say.

My curls are not big, and that's just fine.
No one has curls exactly like mine!

My curls have become just like a friend.
My love for them will never end.

Long and loose, or short and tight,
However I wear my curls is just right.

I let my curls be wild and free.
I love my curls, and my curls love me.

Some say my hair looks messy
and it would look better straight.

But I think they're wrong,
my curly hair is great!

Bouncy, springy, swirly, twirls;
I'm proud of my wonderful curls.

Our Curly Hair Tips

The Pineapple Method: The pineapple method is a hairstyle used to protect curls from frizz and tangles while sleeping. To try this out, gather all of your hair into a loose, high ponytail on top of your head. You can use an elastic band or our favorite...a silk scrunchie to keep your hair secure. When you wake up in the morning, take the pineapple down and refresh your curls. We use a little water and a little product to refresh our curls.

Deep Conditioning: Curls need lots of moisture, so we like to deep condition our curls once a week. After washing our hair *(we only wash our hair once or a few times a week. No need to wash curly hair every day)*, we then apply a deep conditioner in place of our regular conditioner. This can be done in the shower or post-shower. We like to leave our deep conditioner on for fifteen to thirty minutes then rinse out. Deep conditioning *consistently* each week has really helped our curls!

Our Favorite Curly Hair Accessories:
- **Satin or Silk Pillowcases:** Sleeping on a satin or silk pillowcase doesn't create as much friction and helps minimize frizz as you sleep. You can also use a satin bonnet.
- **Silk Scrunchies:** Silk scrunchies are great to use for curly hair because they do not leave any creases or snag the hair.
- **Spray Water Bottle:** A spray water bottle is great to have to help refresh your curls.
- **Hair Pick:** A hair pick is great to use to fluff out your curls and help create more volume.
- **A Microfiber Towel:** A microfiber towel is a great tool to use to help absorb extra water and cut down on drying time. It also helps prevent frizz and doesn't disrupt the curl pattern like regular bath towels can. You can use a cotton T-shirt if you don't have a microfiber towel.

Curly Hair Products:
There are so many products for curly hair...gel, cream, mousse, oil, leave-in conditioner, etc. It's important to find the right products for *your* curls. Some products are made to help with frizz while others are made to help give your curls moisture. Read the labels to see what will work best for your needs.
- Tristan's favorite product for her curls is a strong hold gel because it helps provide hold and frizz control. She likes to apply the gel to wet hair and then let her hair air dry till about eighty percent, and then diffuse it. Once her hair is completely dry, she likes to flip her hair over and *scrunch out the crunch* (SOTC). This helps make Tristan's curls soft and bouncy.
- Lacey's favorite product to use is a mousse because it provides a lightweight hold on her long curls. She prefers mousse because her curls tend to get weighed down easily. She likes to apply the mousse to wet hair and let it air dry till about eighty percent, and then diffuse it.

These are a few tips that we have found helpful for us.

We encourage you to find what works best for your hair and remember to embrace your wonderful curls.

Made in United States
North Haven, CT
15 November 2022

26714133R00015